ZIGGY PIGGY

AND THE
THREE LITTLE PIGS

FRANK ASCH

KIDS CAN PRESS

We acknowledge the support of the Canada Council for the Arts
and the Ontario Arts Council for our publishing program.

Published in Canada by
Kids Can Press Ltd.
29 Birch Avenue
Toronto, ON M4V 1E2

Published in the U.S. by
Kids Can Press Ltd.
85 River Rock Drive, Suite 202
Buffalo, NY 14207

The artwork in this book was drawn in pencil and scanned into Adobe Photoshop 4.0.
Colorization and special effects by Frank and Jan Asch.
Text is set in Palatino.

Edited by Debbie Rogosin
Designed by Julia Naimska
Printed in Hong Kong by Book Art Inc., Toronto

CM 98 0 9 8 7 6 5 4 3 2 1

Canadian Cataloguing in Publication Data

Asch, Frank
Ziggy Piggy and the three little pigs

ISBN 1-55074-515-8

I. Title.

PZ7.A778Zi   1998   j813′.54   C97-932651-6

To that most excellent wolf, Ed Updike.

Once upon a time there were four little pigs. The first little pig lived in a house made of straw. His name was Ted.

The second little pig lived in a house made of sticks.
His name was Fred.

The third little pig lived in a house made of bricks.
His name was Ned.

The fourth little pig didn't have a house at all. He slept outdoors under the stars. His name was Ziggy.

One day Ziggy went to visit his brother Ted.
"I just stopped by to see if you wanted to go for a swim," said Ziggy.

"Haven't you heard?" said Ted. "There's a Big Bad Wolf in town! I have to stay home and put a new lock on my door. If you were smart you wouldn't be thinking about swimming. You'd be building a house like mine to keep you safe and sound."

"You're probably right," said Ziggy, "but I really want to go swimming today." And he went down the road to visit his brother Fred.

Fred had also heard about the Big Bad Wolf. He was busy installing bars across his windows when Ziggy came into the yard and asked him to go swimming.

"Swimming!" cried Fred. "If I were you I'd stay here until the Big Bad Wolf moves on."

"Thanks for the offer," said Ziggy. "But it's too nice a day to be indoors."

"Have it your way," said Fred. "Just don't say I never warned you."

On his way to the beach, Ziggy stopped at Ned's house. Ned was putting a grate on his chimney.

"What's that for?" called Ziggy.

"It's just a little extra Big Bad Wolf protection. They've been known to come down chimneys, you know. But this grate is guaranteed wolf-proof."

"I don't imagine you'd be interested in going for a swim today," said Ziggy.

"No way," said Ned.

So Ziggy went swimming alone.

While Ziggy splashed and built sandcastles on the beach, the Big Bad Wolf went to visit Ted.

"Open your door or I'll huff and I'll puff and I'll blow your house in," declared the Big Bad Wolf.

"Not by the hair on my chinny chin chin!" replied Ted.

So the Big Bad Wolf huffed and puffed and blew Ted's house in.

"Help! Help!" cried Ted, and he ran to Fred's house.

Of course the Big Bad Wolf followed him.

"Open your door or I'll huff and I'll puff and I'll blow your house in," said the Big Bad Wolf.

"Not by the hair on our chinny chin chins," replied Ted and Fred.

So the Big Bad Wolf huffed and puffed and blew Fred's house in.

"Hurry, let's go to Ned's house!" shouted Fred.

When Ted and Fred arrived, Ned said, "Don't worry.
You'll be safe here."

"Are you sure?" asked Ted and Fred.

"Of course I am," chuckled Ned. "No one can blow down
a house made of bricks!"

Then they heard the voice of the Big Bad Wolf.

"Open your door or I'll huff and I'll puff and I'll blow your house in," he bellowed.

"Not by the hair on our chinny chin chins!" cried the three little pigs.

"And don't think you can come down the chimney either, because I fixed that!" added Ned.

So the Big Bad Wolf took a deep breath, and he huffed and he puffed and he puffed and he huffed and he blew Ned's house in!

"Now what?" squealed Ted.
"Beats me!" said Ned. "This has never happened before."
"Run for your lives!" cried Fred.

The three little pigs ran and ran until they came to the beach. Ziggy wasn't swimming anymore. After building sandcastles he had made a raft out of driftwood. Now he was sunning himself and watching the clouds drift by.

"He's coming!" shouted Ted.

"Who's coming?" asked Ziggy.

"The Big Bad Wolf!" said Fred. "He's going to eat us for breakfast, lunch and dinner!"

"And *you'll* be his midnight snack," said Ned.

"Quick! Hop aboard my raft," said Ziggy.

"What good will that do?" asked Ted. "If he can blow down a house made of bricks, he can surely blow your raft to smithereens!"

"Just do what I say, and let me do the talking," said Ziggy.

So the three little pigs swam out to Ziggy's raft.

Just then, the Big Bad Wolf appeared on the beach, only slightly out of breath.

"Come off that raft or I'll huff and I'll puff and I'll blow it to pieces!" said the Big Bad Wolf.

"You talk big," said Ziggy. "But I doubt you're wolf
enough to blow out a birthday candle!"

"Oh yeah? Well, we'll see about that," said the
Big Bad Wolf. And he huffed and he puffed and he puffed
and he huffed.

At that very moment, Ziggy raised the sail of his raft.

So when the Big Bad Wolf finally blew,

he blew the tiny raft far out to sea.

At last the four little pigs were safe and sound!
"We sure are glad you went to the beach today,"
said Ted, Fred and Ned.
"Me too!" said Ziggy.
And they all went for a swim!